DANIEL TIGER'S NEIGHBORHOOD®

Daniel Visits the Library

adapted by Maggie Testa
based on the screenplay "Calm for Storytime"
written by Wendy Harris
poses and layouts by Jason Fruchter

Ready-to-Read

Simon Spotlight
New York   London   Toronto   Sydney   New Delhi

SIMON SPOTLIGHT
An imprint of Simon & Schuster Children's Publishing Division
1230 Avenue of the Americas, New York, New York 10020
This Simon Spotlight edition August 2015
© 2015 The Fred Rogers Company.
For information about special discounts for bulk purchases, please contact Simon & Schuster Special Sales at
1-866-506-1949 or business@simonandschuster.com.
Manufactured in the United States of America 0715 LAK
2 4 6 8 10 9 7 5 3 1
ISBN 978-1-4814-4173-5 (hc)
ISBN 978-1-4814-4172-8 (pbk)
ISBN 978-1-4814-4174-2 (eBook)

Hi, neighbor!
We are going to the
library for storytime.

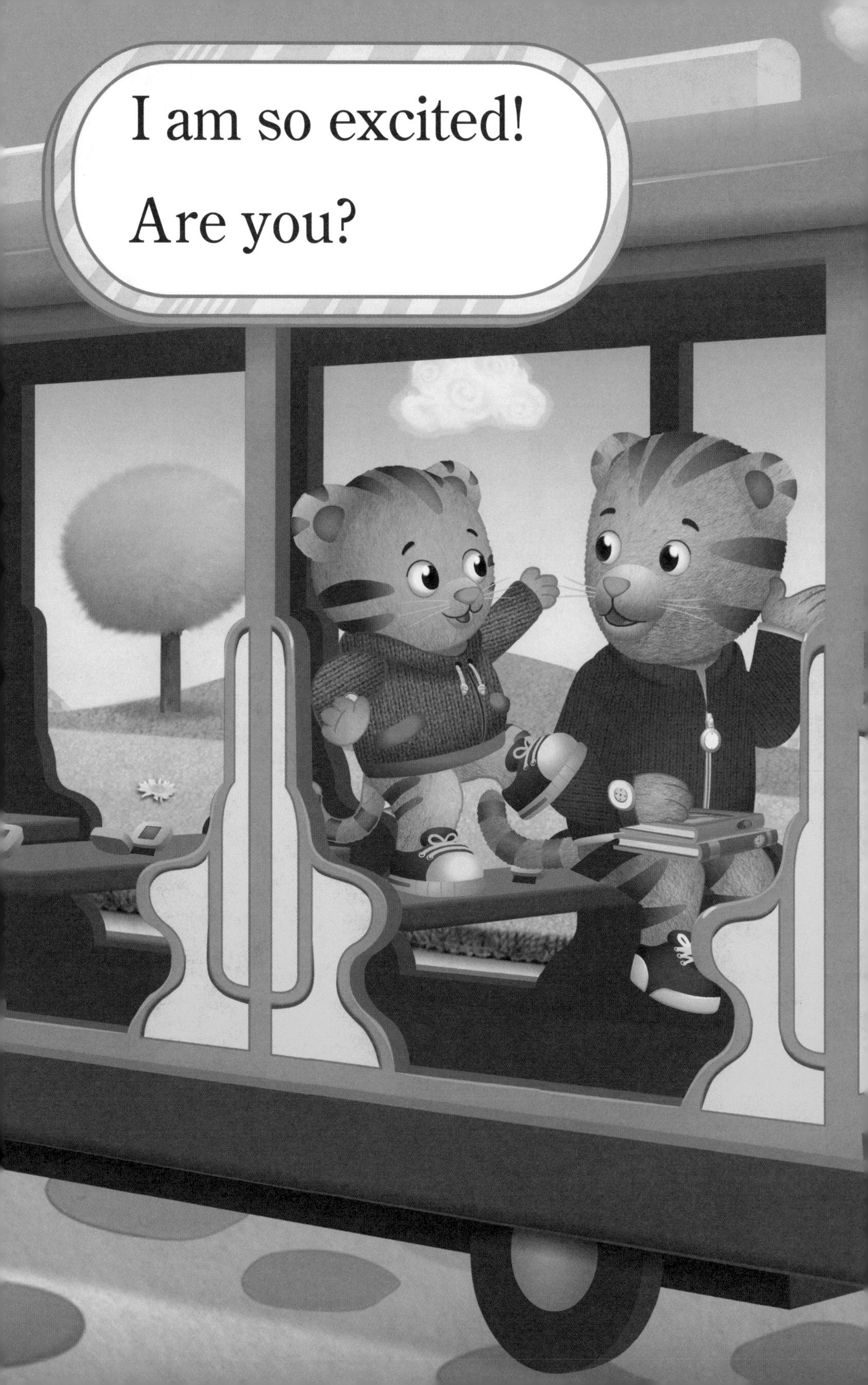

I am so excited!

Are you?

"Trolley cannot go until you are calm," says Dad.

Give a squeeze,
nice and slow.

Take a deep breath and let it go.

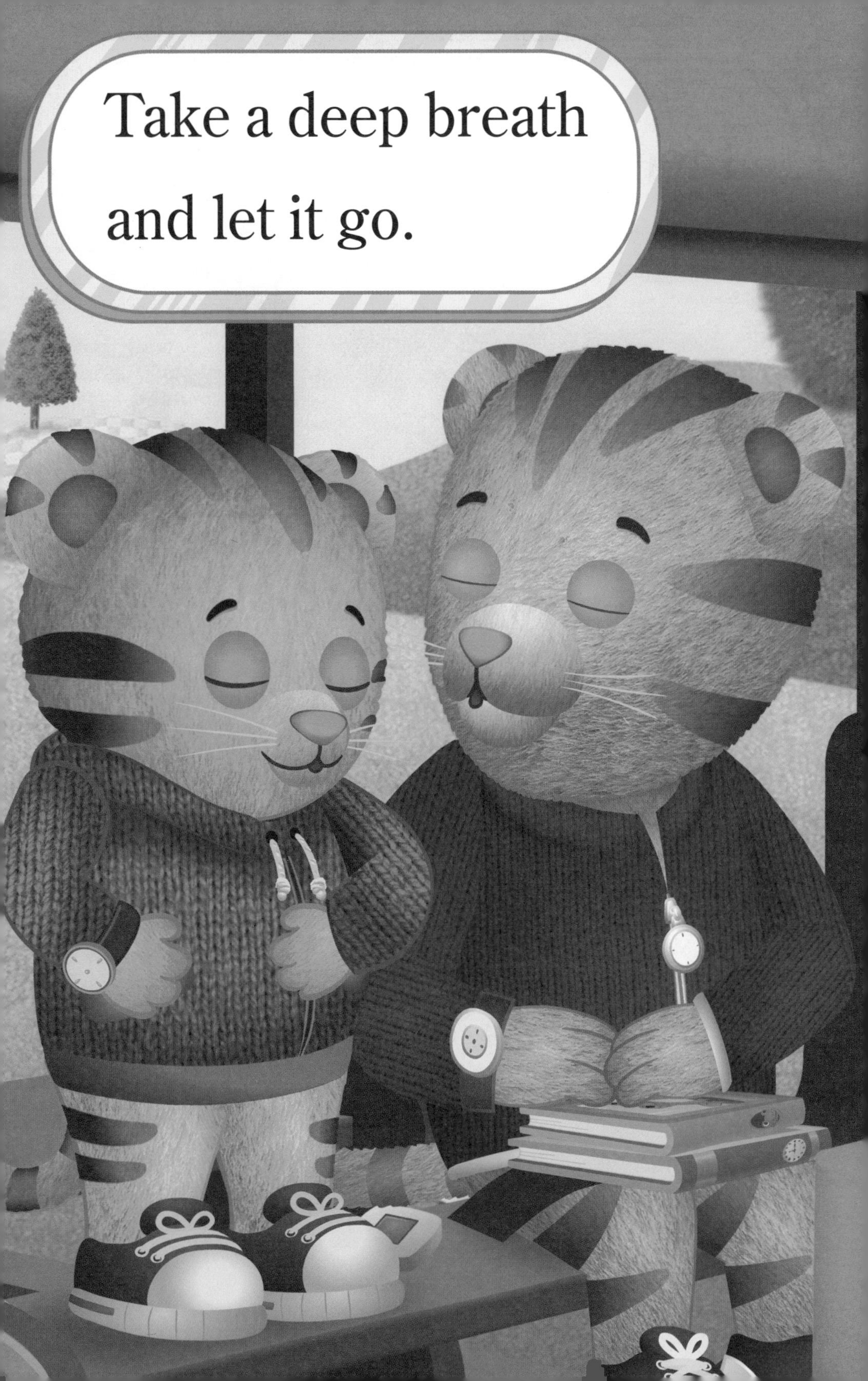

"Hoo! Hoo! Hello," says O the Owl.

X the Owl reads a book to us.

Prince Wednesday hops like a frog.

"Ribbit, ribbit," he says.

I cannot hear the story.

"Storytime is a time to be quiet and calm," says X the Owl.

Do you know how we can help Prince Wednesday feel calm?

Take a deep breath and let it go.

We listen to the story.

X the Owl finishes the story.

"The end," he says.

Storytime is over.
Now we can go
outside and play.

Have you ever wanted to be calm when you were excited?

Next time that happens, you know what to do.